Puppy Love Prank

Don't miss a single
Nancy Drew
Clue Book:

Nancy Drew

* CLUE BOOK *

#13

Puppy Love Prank

BY CAROLYN KEENE * ILLUSTRATED BY PETER FRANCIS

Aladdin

NEW YORK   LONDON   TORONTO   SYDNEY   NEW DELHI

ALADDIN

An imprint of Simon & Schuster Children's Publishing Division
1230 Avenue of the Americas, New York, New York 10020
First Aladdin paperback edition March 2020
Text copyright © 2020 by Simon & Schuster, Inc.
Illustrations copyright © 2020 by Peter Francis
NANCY DREW, NANCY DREW CLUE BOOK,
and colophons are registered trademarks of Simon & Schuster, Inc.
Also available in an Aladdin hardcover edition.
All rights reserved, including the right of reproduction in whole or in part in any form.
ALADDIN and related logo are registered trademarks of Simon & Schuster, Inc.
For information about special discounts for bulk purchases, please contact Simon & Schuster
Special Sales at 1-866-506-1949 or business@simonandschuster.com.
The Simon & Schuster Speakers Bureau can bring authors to your live event.
For more information or to book an event contact the Simon & Schuster Speakers Bureau
at 1-866-248-3049 or visit our website at www.simonspeakers.com.
Series designed by Karina Granda
Cover designed by Heather Palisi
Interior designed by Tom Daly
The illustrations for this book were rendered digitally.
The text of this book was set in Adobe Garamond Pro.
Manufactured in the United States of America 0220 OFF
2 4 6 8 10 9 7 5 3 1
Library of Congress Cataloging-in-Publication Data
Names: Keene, Carolyn, author. | Francis, Peter, 1973– illustrator.
Title: Puppy love prank / by Carolyn Keene ; illustrated by Peter Francis.
Description: First Aladdin hardcover/paperback edition. | New York : Aladdin, 2020. | Series: Nancy
Drew clue book ; [13] | Summary: As attendants at the wedding of wealthy Mrs. Ainsworth's dogs,
Nancy Drew and her friends Bess and George investigate how the bride and groom got tie-dyed.
Identifiers: LCCN 2018059749 (print) | LCCN 2018061190 (eBook) |
ISBN 9781534431355 (eBook) | ISBN 9781534431331 (pbk) | ISBN 9781534431348 (hc)
Subjects: | CYAC: Weddings—Fiction. | Bichon frise—Fiction. | Dogs—Fiction. |
Mystery and detective stories.
Classification: LCC PZ7.K23 (eBook) | LCC PZ7.K23 Pup 2020 (print) | DDC [Fic]—dc23
LC record available at https://lccn.loc.gov/2018059749

* CONTENTS *

Chapter

TAIL-WAGGING WEDDING

"Stop!" Bess Marvin shouted as she came to a halt. "We forgot something super important!"

Nancy Drew stopped walking too. So did her other best friend, George Fayne. All three girls were carrying plastic bins filled with treats for the wedding they were going to today.

"We didn't forget to dress up for the wedding," Nancy told Bess. "We're both wearing party dresses and George is wearing a button-up shirt."

"Yes, but every wedding has something old,

something new, something borrowed, and something blue," Bess explained. "We don't have any of those."

George raised a foot and said, "My sneakers are old."

Bess rolled her eyes at George's grubby, frayed sneaker. "That's for sure," she sighed.

"And I'm wearing Hannah's sparkly poodle pin," Nancy said. "That's borrowed."

"Your dress is new, Bess," George said, "like everything else you wear."

"Very funny," Bess said with a smirk.

Nancy giggled. She had known Bess and George forever but still couldn't believe they were cousins.

Bess washed her long blond hair almost every morning, painted her nails pink, and had a closet filled with stylin' clothes. The only time George trimmed her nails was when they grew too long for her computer keyboard or softball catcher's mitt.

But like Nancy, Bess and George were great at

solving mysteries. That's why all three friends had their own detective club called the Clue Crew. Nancy even had a special notebook where she wrote down all their suspects and clues!

"We need something blue, you guys," Bess insisted. "It's a wedding tradition."

George's dark curls bounced as she shook her head. "It's a dog wedding, Bess," she pointed out. "There's nothing traditional about that."

Nancy, Bess, and George stood outside Mayor Strong's mansion, where the dog wedding would take place. Getting married were Helga and Horatio, the fluffy white bichon frises of Mrs. Ainsworth, the richest woman in River Heights.

"Let's not forget the main reason for this wedding," Nancy said. "To let everyone know about the pet shelter Waggamuffins and all the dogs who need homes."

"And because my mom is catering the wedding," George said proudly. "We get to walk three of those dogs down the aisles as brides-mutts. How cool is that?"

"It would be even cooler," Bess sighed, "if we could find something blue."

Nancy, Bess, and George carried the bins filled with doggy cupcakes up the path to the mayor's mansion. Mrs. Fayne and her staff unloaded the catering truck to one side of the driveway.

When Mrs. Fayne saw the girls, she smiled. "Thanks for bringing the pupcakes, girls," she said. "You can put the bins on the rolling cart."

"Good," George said with a grin. "These cupcakes may be for dogs, but there're enough to feed ten elephants!"

"Where are Helga and Horatio, Mrs. Fayne?" Nancy asked while stacking the bins. "We'd love to meet them before the wedding!"

"Mayor Strong arranged a special room for the dogs," Mrs. Fayne said, pointing to a door at the back of the house. "It even has its own entrance."

Mrs. Fayne returned to her work and the girls turned toward the door. Nancy brushed aside her reddish-blond bangs to read a sign on the door. It read: PRIVATE.

"Now we can't go inside the room to meet Helga and Horatio," Nancy said, disappointed.

"Who says we can't?" George asked. She walked to the rolling cart, grabbed two pup-cakes, and said, "Special delivery for Helga and Horatio!"

Nancy knocked three times on the door. They waited until a woman's voice called, "Enter!"

Bess opened the door. As they stepped inside, the girls looked around the room. The first things they noticed were a doggy-size wedding dress and tuxedo hanging on a rack. Standing by the rack and waving a steamer was a boy of about nine or ten.

A silver-haired woman sat on a velvet throne-like chair holding two fluffy white dogs. "You missed a wrinkle on the left suspender, Ludlow," she told the boy. "Keep steaming, please."

"Yes, Grandma," Ludlow replied.

Nancy guessed the woman was Mrs. Ainsworth. The dogs had to be Helga and Horatio!

"Hello, Mrs. Ainsworth," Nancy said. "We've

come with pupcakes for the happy couple. They're cupcakes baked for dogs—"

"Not these dogs," Mrs. Ainsworth cut in. "What would my babies do if they got cream on their clean fur?"

"They'd lick it off," George said with a shrug. "They're dogs, right?"

Mrs. Ainsworth didn't laugh, but Ludlow did. He blushed when he noticed Nancy, Bess, and George looking his way.

"Do you go to River Heights Elementary School?" Nancy asked nicely. "You don't look familiar."

"That's because I live in the next town," Ludlow said, turning off the steamer. "I'm helping my grandmother with the wedding."

"And making sure my babies stay perfectly groomed on their big day," Mrs. Ainsworth added.

"Did someone say 'groomed'?" a voice piped in.

Nancy, Bess, and George turned to see a couple at the door. Each wore a crisp smock over tailored pants. They carried branded tote bags over their shoulders.

"And you are?" Mrs. Ainsworth asked.

"I'm Kelly Davis and this is my husband Kevin," the woman said, "Better known as the Va-Va-Groom glam squad!"

"I know what a glam squad is," Bess said excitedly. "You make people beautiful, right?"

"We make dogs beautiful," Kevin stated.

"Va-Va-Groom is the fancy new dog salon on Main Street," Kelly added.

"I heard about Va-Va-Groom," Nancy said. "It's way too fancy for my dog, Chip."

In a flash Kelly handed Nancy a piece of paper and said, "Take this coupon. It's for twenty dollars off a soothing sports pawdicure including tax and tip."

"Pawdicure?" Nancy asked.

"Now," Kelly said, smiling at Helga and Horatio. "Where do we begin?"

"By leaving, please," Mrs. Ainsworth said. "I never called for groomers."

"That's because I did!" Mayor Strong boomed as he burst into the room following a huge hairy dog. "For my dog, Huey."

Nancy wanted to squeeze her nose but didn't. Huey smelled a bit ewie. Meanwhile the glam squad stared at the mayor's dog.

"Would your dog like a soothing massage, Mayor Strong?" Kevin asked. "Or colorful stencils on his rather matted fur?"

"Nah," Mayor Strong said. "Huey rolled in

something stinky. Dig out the dead leaves or whatever else you find in there."

The mayor gave his dog a final pat. "Oh, and clean the gunk out of his ears, too. So he can hear me whistle."

Nancy could tell the glam squad was horrified by the mayor's request. In a panic the couple turned to Mrs. Ainsworth.

"Surely there's something we can do for the bride and groom!" Kelly said. "Instead of Huey?"

"Pleeeeease?" Kevin squeaked.

"I'm afraid not," Mrs. Ainsworth said. "Helga and Horatio were groomed this morning by Mr. Clippy of Canine Couture."

"You mean the celebrity dog groomer to the stars?" Kelly gasped. "His salon is in Chicago!"

"Mr. Clippy makes house calls," Mrs. Ainsworth said, "in his private helicopter."

Nancy could hear Kelly and Kevin growl under their breaths. Just like the dogs they groomed.

"I'll leave Huey in your good hands," Mayor Strong said, sticking the leash between Kelly's

clenched fingers. "See you all at the wedding!"

Kelly and Kevin stood frozen as the mayor left the room. George turned to the couple. "Take these for Huey," she said, holding out the two pupcakes. "I'm sure he won't mind frosting on his fur."

"It would be an improvement," Kevin muttered.

"Woof!" Huey barked.

Kelly steered Huey toward the door. On their

way out Nancy heard her say, "Kevin, I think we've just been dogged!"

Nancy didn't know what Kelly meant by that. But she did know one thing: The Va-Va-Groom glam squad was mad!

"Should I shut the door, Grandma?" Ludlow asked.

"Don't bother, dear," Mrs. Ainsworth said. "It's eleven o'clock and time for you to walk Helga and Horatio."

Nancy, Bess, and George listened to Mrs. Ainsworth give Ludlow special walking instructions: Walk Helga and Horatio for a half an hour away from the guests. Then bring the dogs back to their room for an hour's rest before the wedding at twelve thirty.

While Ludlow fetched the dogs' leashes, Nancy had an idea. . . .

"Why don't you walk Helga and Horatio in the park across the street, Ludlow?" Nancy asked. "My dog, Chip, loves it there!"

"The park?" Mrs. Ainsworth demanded. "Do

my babies look like they chase squirrels?"

Suddenly—MEOW! Nancy, Bess, and George whirled around. Standing in the doorway was a cat wearing a ruffled collar and lacy bonnet. Helga and Horatio growled at the little cat, then leaped off of Mrs. Ainsworth's lap. Yapping all the way, the dogs chased the cat out the door!

"They may not chase squirrels," George exclaimed, pointing outside. "But look at them go after that cat!"

Mrs. Ainsworth jumped up from her chair, wringing her hands. "I told Mayor Strong not to invite cats to this wedding! Somebody bring back my babies!"

Chapter

BRIDE AND GLOOM

"On it, Mrs. Ainsworth!" Nancy said.

With Ludlow running behind them, Nancy, Bess, and George chased the dogs that chased the cat. They charged through the mayor's garden, beneath a lawn sprinkler, and through Mrs. Fayne's catering tent.

"Whoa!" George shouted as the three animals scampered under the table holding the wedding cake. The tall cake decorated with a dog-couple topper trembled this way and that, but luckily didn't fall.

Helga and Horatio chased the cat out of the tent. Ludlow caught up with the dogs, snapping on their leashes and shouting, "Gotcha!"

Ludlow hurried off with both dogs. Meowing, the cat jumped into the open arms of a girl dressed in a fancy dress and straw hat. "There you are, Cocoa," she cooed. "I was wondering where you went!"

Nancy, Bess, and George recognized the girl and her two friends, who walked over carrying cats too.

The three were in the fourth grade and best friends because of their love of cats. They even gave themselves cat nicknames to prove it: Kitty McNulty, Ally Katz, and Purr-cilla Chang. Everyone at school called them the Kitty Klub!

"Your cats look so pretty in their frilly collars and bonnets!" Bess said with a smile.

The Kitty Klub refused to smile back.

"Mayor Strong just told us that cats aren't allowed at the wedding," Kitty said.

"We want to know why," Ally demanded.

"I know why," George replied. "Cats plus dogs equal zoomies. You just saw for yourself."

"But we got something from the registry list!" Purr-cilla complained, holding a chew toy with her free hand. She gave it a squeak and said, "See?"

"Sorry," Nancy said gently. "But Mrs. Ainsworth, Helga and Horatio's owner, said the same."

The Kitty Klub traded frowns.

"Who ever heard of a dog wedding, anyway?" Kitty grumbled as they turned to leave.

"Yeah, well, somebody is about to hear from us," Purr-cilla said, "because I just got an idea!"

The Kitty Klub huddled together, talking quietly as they walked away.

"I wonder what Purr-cilla's idea is," Nancy said.

"To have a cat wedding?" Bess guessed with a smile.

"Whatever." Nancy giggled. "I just hope Ludlow holds those leashes tight during the dogs' walk. Helga and Horatio will take off again the minute they see a squirrel!"

"You mean like that one?" Bess asked.

She pointed to a squirrel zooming across the lawn. The bushy-tailed critter rammed into a rock, flipping onto its back. A loud whirring noise rose from the squirrel as his feet kicked in the air.

"That's not a real squirrel," George said. "It's electronic."

"Coming through!" a boy shouted. He ran to the squirrel, picked it up, and turned a switch on its stomach. The creature stopped whirring and kicking.

The boy was Bradley Bishop, from the other third grade class at school. More than anything Bradley loved to invent, and was good at it too. He even had his own YouView channel called Bradley's Brainstorms, where he showed off his latest inventions.

"What are you doing here, Bradley?" Nancy

asked. "Did you get an invitation to the dog wedding?"

"Bradley Bishop needs no invitation!" Bradley declared. "Surely Mrs. Ainsworth will be interested in seeing my latest brainstorms."

"Like an electronic squirrel?" George cried.

"This bushy-tailed brainstorm is perfect for Helga and Horatio to chase down the aisle," Bradley explained.

"I think Helga and Horatio prefer cats," Bess said, and giggled.

"I also have a rice blaster so guests don't have to throw rice," Bradley went on. "Plus a canine cake slicer made to cut perfect dog-size slices."

Bradley puffed his chest out proudly and said, "Or my latest invention, the Bradley Bishop Blaster Booth."

"My mom already ordered a photo booth," George said.

"It's not a photo booth!" Bradley insisted. "I live around the corner—come over and see it."

"Thanks, but no thanks," George said.

"We have a wedding to go to," Nancy said.

As the girls walked away, Bradley shouted after them, "How can it be a wedding without Bradley's Brainstorms?"

Nancy, Bess, and George had a great time meeting the Waggamuffins shelter dogs they would walk down the aisle.

Each dog wore a garland or bow tie around their neck and a bib that read TAKE ME HOME.

Time flew as the girls said hi to more dogs in the Waggamuffins truck parked outside the

mansion. Soon it was twelve thirty and time for the wedding!

"You rehearsed last night," a wedding volunteer told Nancy, Bess, and George with a smile. "So you know the drill."

The girls formed a line with their dogs outside the ballroom where the ceremony was about to begin. From behind the double doors they could hear a string quartet play a song called "Puppy Love."

"This is it!" Nancy whispered excitedly.

Two ushers pulled open the doors. Nancy's heart fluttered as she looked inside the ballroom. Seated on both sides of a long, satiny aisle were guests, all smiling her way!

Nancy walked down the aisle first, escorting Barkley. The medium-size Bossi-Poo was part Boston terrier, part poodle. Next in walked George leading a lively Doodleman pinscher named Knuckles, followed by Bess with Dahlia—a tiny Pom-huahua.

Standing at the end of the aisle was a grinning

Mayor Strong. At his side was Huey, still looking scruffy.

Nancy, Bess, and George took their places alongside the mayor with the dogs. As the orchestra played "Here Comes the Bride," all eyes turned toward the doors. But where were the bride and groom?

That's when—

"Eeeeek!"

Everyone gasped, some standing up as a frantic Mrs. Ainsworth charged down the aisle. Helga was in one arm, Horatio in the other. Mrs. Ainsworth was fancily dressed, but neither dog wore their wedding attire. Instead the snowy-white pups wore wild streaks of color all over their fur!

"Omigosh!" Nancy cried to her friends. "The groom and bride are tie-dyed!"

Chapter

3

TIE-DYE THE KNOT

The whole ballroom was in an uproar as guests crowded around the color-splashed canines.

"I think we found something blue for the wedding, Bess," George whispered. "Blue, green, yellow, purple—"

"Not. Funny. George," Bess insisted. She gripped the leash tightly as Dahlia became jittery. "Even the Waggamuffins dogs are upset."

"Not as upset as Mrs. Ainsworth," Nancy said.

Mrs. Ainsworth broke out of the crowd,

having overheard Nancy. "You bet I'm upset!" she screeched. "I was busy getting dressed and bejeweled for the wedding. Five minutes before the ceremony I went into my babies' room and found them like this!"

She turned to Ludlow and asked, "How did this happen? You were the last to see Helga and Horatio before you put them down for their nap."

"And when I did, their fur was totally clean," Ludlow insisted. "I don't know how that happened, Grandma!"

Mayor Strong told Huey to stay, then walked over to Mrs. Ainsworth. "Lola," he told her soothingly, "I'm sure there's a reasonable explanation for this . . . color conundrum."

The mayor then turned to the guests and said, "Okay, everybody. Who doodled on the poodles?"

"They're not poodles, they're bichon frises!" Mrs. Ainsworth cried. "But you're right about one thing: Someone in this mansion painted my pooches!"

At that moment Mrs. Fayne walked into the ballroom. Not realizing what had happened, she announced with a smile, "Attention, everyone. Helga and Horatio's wedding cake is now being served in the dining room!"

"There will be nothing of the kind," Mrs. Ainsworth snapped.

"Excuse me?" Mrs. Fayne asked, until she saw Helga and Horatio. "Holy cannoli!"

Still clutching her dogs, Mrs. Ainsworth turned to Mayor Strong. "I am calling off Helga and Horatio's wedding immediately," she declared, "plus my support of Waggamuffins, until the dastardly dog dappler comes forward!"

Everyone in the ballroom looked shocked as Mrs. Ainsworth huffed out of the ballroom with Helga and Horatio. Rushing after her was Ludlow.

The musicians began playing "The Party's Over" while Mrs. Fayne whisked stunned guests out of the ballroom.

Nancy, Bess, and George handed the leashes

to the Waggamuffins volunteers. They then followed the other guests out of the ballroom and outside.

"If Mrs. Ainsworth doesn't support Waggamufffins, it could shut down," Bess said sadly. "Who else will take care of the shelter dogs until they find homes?"

"Waggamuffins needs all the help they can get," George said.

"They sure do," Nancy said with a nod. "And they are about to get it."

Bess smiled as she read Nancy's thoughts. "You mean this is a case for the Clue Crew?" she asked.

"I know you carry your clue book everywhere, Nancy," George said. "But even to weddings?"

"Let's just say, I do!" Nancy said, pulling her clue book from her satiny waist pouch. "We have to find who color-coated Helga and Horatio, so Mrs. Ainsworth will support Waggamuffins."

By now the Waggamuffins trailer had driven away. Mrs. Fayne and her staff were loading food back into the catering van. Mrs. Fayne drove her van everywhere, even to George's soccer games.

George pulled her soccer ball from the van and began kicking it around. Nancy and Bess sat down on a garden bench.

"Do you have to kick that ball now, George?" Bess called to her cousin. "We've got a mystery to solve."

"Kicking helps me think," George called back, bouncing the ball on her foot. "So what do we know so far?"

Nancy opened her clue book on her lap.

Tucked inside was a bright green pen with a daisy design—perfect for spring!

"Mrs. Ainsworth found Helga and Horatio in their room, already covered with paint," Nancy began. "That's where the crime probably took place."

"But *when* did it take place?" Bess asked.

George bounced the soccer ball on her knee. "Let's do the math," she said. "Mrs. Ainsworth told Ludlow to walk her dogs at eleven o'clock and bring them back at eleven thirty to rest."

"How did you remember that?" Nancy asked.

"My stomach starts growling between eleven and lunchtime," George said, chasing the soccer ball. "Which reminds me, when I got my soccer ball from my mom's van, I grabbed some snacks!"

The girls took a short lunch break to eat flattened sandwich wraps that had been stuffed inside George's pocket. They then got back to work.

Tapping her chin with the tip of her pen always helped Nancy think. "Helga and Horatio's wedding was to start at twelve thirty," she said.

"I'm thinking that Ludlow brought the dogs back sometime around eleven thirty," George said, giving the ball a kick. "The pooch-painter must have struck between eleven thirty and twelve thirty."

Nancy wrote the timeline in her clue book. Next she turned to a fresh page and wrote the word "Suspects."

"Okay, who would have done such a thing to Helga and Horatio?"

"Someone might have been mad about the wedding," Bess figured. "So they painted the bride and groom to make Mrs. Ainsworth mad too."

"I'd be mad too if my dogs looked like spin art!" George said.

"You've got to admit," Bess said with a smile, "those colors did make Helga and Horatio kind of glam."

Glam! The word made Nancy's eyes light up.

"You guys," Nancy said, "the glam squad from Va-Va-Groom was mad that they couldn't groom Helga and Horatio."

"But they had another job," George said. "Grooming Huey before the wedding."

"Huey still looked grubby at the wedding," Bess pointed out. "As if he wasn't groomed at all."

"The glam squad mentioned stencils and fur paint," Nancy said. "Maybe there was paint in the bags they were carrying!"

"Which they used on Helga and Horatio!" Bess said excitedly. "Clue Crew—we have our first suspects!"

Nancy began her suspect list with the Va-Va-Groom glam squad at the top. She looked up from her book and asked, "Who else could have painted the dogs?"

"Good question!" George said, giving her ball

a kick. This time it soared through the air, touching down at the far end of the lawn.

George was about to run for it when Kitty, Ally, and Purr-cilla walked around from the back. The Kitty Klub no longer held their cats.

"I got it!" Ally yelled, picking up the ball. With a smile she threw it back to George.

"Good throw, Ally!" George called. "Do you guys want to play?"

The Kitty Klub kept on walking. Nancy noticed that Kitty was wearing a bulky backpack. It was red with a black-and-white cat design.

"Sorry, we have to go," Kitty called back to them over her shoulder.

"What's the hurry?" Bess asked.

"We're going to Mr. Stanley's Wows and Meows Cat Circus," Purr-cilla said. "It's going to be so awesome!"

As Nancy watched the Kitty Klub walk away from the mansion, something didn't add up. . . .

"If Kitty, Ally, and Purr-cilla brought home

their cats, why did they come back to the mansion?" Nancy asked. "And why was Kitty wearing such a big backpack?"

"And why," George asked slowly, "is my soccer ball suddenly covered with colors?"

Chapter

CAT-ASTROPHE

The girls studied the once-plain soccer ball now streaked with color.

"How did those colors get there?" Bess gasped.

"Probably from Ally's hands," Nancy said. "She was the one who picked up the ball and threw it back."

George pointed to a vivid splotch on the ball. "That looks like a handprint to me," she said. "Do you think the Kitty Klub painted Helga and Horatio?"

"Maybe!" Bess replied. "The Kitty Klub was mad because cats weren't allowed at the wedding."

"I heard Purr-cilla say she had an idea," Nancy said. "Maybe color-coating the dogs was it!"

"How would we know for sure?" Bess asked.

"Kitty was wearing a backpack," George said. "Too bad we can't look inside it for jars of paint."

"Who says we can't?" Nancy asked. "I hope you guys like cotton candy, because we're going to the circus. Mr. Stanley's Cat Circus!"

Nancy, Bess, and George found Mrs. Fayne in the mansion kitchen, still packing up leftover food. She let them use her laptop to look up the cat circus.

"The theater is on Walker Street," George said as they studied the website. "Today's circus starts in ten minutes."

"Ten minutes?" Nancy said. "We'd have to run to make it there on time."

"I can drive you there now," Mrs. Fayne said. "You'll have to squeeze into the van. It's loaded with food from the wedding that never was."

Mrs. Fayne held a small bag out to Nancy. "I packed some pupcakes for your dog, Chocolate Chip," she said with a smile.

"Thanks, Mrs. Fayne!" Nancy said, taking the bag.

"How about human cupcakes for us, Mom?" George asked. "I know you baked a batch for the wedding."

"I had those cupcakes brought to the park across the street," Mrs. Fayne explained. "A girl is having her birthday party there, and six-year-olds love cupcakes."

"So do eight-year-olds, Aunt Louise," Bess said. She pointed to a plastic container on the counter. "And since I love tuna fish, too—"

"Help yourself, Bess." Mrs. Louise chuckled.

Mrs. Fayne drove the Clue Crew to Walker Street and the theater where the cat circus would be held. Nancy held the bag of pupcakes. Bess rested the leftover tuna container on her lap.

Once on Walker Street, the girls climbed out of the van. After thanking Mrs. Fayne they walked toward the small, old-timey building with the theater's address.

"That's a theater?" Bess asked, surprised. "It looks more like an old store!"

"It's a cat circus, Bess," George said. "Not a Broadway show!"

A man sat outside the theater, selling the tickets. Mrs. Fayne had given each girl some money for the cat circus and for helping out at the dog wedding.

"Three tickets, please," Nancy said.

The man pointed at the bag and container. "No food during the show, girls," he said. "You'll have to put that in the cubbies once you're inside."

"We will, thank you," Nancy said.

The girls filed through the door into the theater. The carpeting in the lobby smelled musty—like a closet that hadn't been opened in a long, long time.

"Let's put away the food and then look for Kitty, Ally, and Purr-cilla," Nancy told her friends as they headed for the thick velvet curtain leading inside. "Bess, you talk to them. George, you go through the backpack to look for paint."

"Why do I always get the dirty work?" George asked.

Bess nodded at George's grubby sneakers. "Do you have to ask?"

The girls slipped through the curtain into the dark theater. All that was lit was the stage. It was already filled with cats wearing costumes and playing musical instruments.

"The show has started!" Bess whispered.

A tiger cat was using a stick in his mouth to beat on a set of drums. Another cat of the Persian variety plucked the strings of a guitar while an energetic Tabby played the xylophone.

Also onstage was a man dressed in a black top hat and green jacket. Nancy guessed he was Mr. Stanley.

"How do you like our house band, kids?" he asked the audience. "Or as our musicians would prefer—mouse band!"

"Corny," George whispered. "And it's too dark in here to see Kitty, Ally, and Purr-cilla."

"What should we do, Nancy?" Bess asked, keeping her voice low.

"Let's put the food in the cubbies first," Nancy said. "Then we'll figure out what to do."

Nancy found a cubby shelf along the back wall. But George found more. Stuffed inside one cubby was Kitty's backpack!

"Check it out!" George hissed, pointing to it. "Are we lucky or what?"

"We'll be luckier if we find a clue," Nancy

whispered. "Let's look inside the backpack for cans of paint."

Kitty's backpack was a tight fit. Nancy pulled and pulled to get it out of the cubby. Until—

"Oof!" Nancy grunted as the backpack popped out. Still in her hands, it flipped upside down, sending three cans spilling to the floor with a loud clatter!

Jumping back from the rolling cans, George crashed into Bess. The container flew out of Bess's hands and hit the floor. The lid popped off and a huge lump of tuna popped out!

"Look what you did, George!" Bess wailed. "You made me lose my tuna!"

"Okay, but look what we found," George said, pointing to the floor. "I'll bet those are cans of paint!"

The music screeched to a sudden stop. The girls turned to see Mr. Stanley's cat band still onstage. Instead of playing their instruments they stared toward the back of the theater, their bright cat eyes glowing in the dark.

"What are they looking at?" Nancy whispered.

"Not looking," George said with a frown. "Smelling!"

The house lights flashed on and—"Meow! Meow! Meeeeeooooow!"

The cat band—plus every cat waiting in the wings—began running and leaping toward the dropped lump of tuna. Audience members shrieked as hungry cats climbed over their shoulders and heads to get to the fish!

"Hey!" Ally shouted from her seat. "Isn't that Nancy, Bess, and George back there?"

"I didn't know they liked cats," Purr-cilla said. "What are they doing here?"

"I have a better question!" Kitty said, narrowing her eyes. "Why is Nancy Drew holding my backpack?"

Nancy gulped at the backpack still in her hands.

Awkward!

Chapter

5

SIDEWALK TALK

"Get back, get back!" Mr. Stanley shouted at the cats. "Your set isn't over yet!"

While the cats feasted on tuna, the Kitty Klub marched up to Nancy, Bess, and George.

"If you're looking for candy in my backpack, you're so out of luck," Kitty told Nancy. "My mom won't let me eat sweets."

"We weren't looking for candy," Nancy said, "but we *were* looking for clues."

"Helga and Horatio were color-splashed right

before their wedding!" Bess shouted over ear-splitting meows. "You were mad that cats weren't allowed."

"So you used cans of spray paint to get even," George said, pointing to the floor.

The Kitty Klub appeared totally confused as they stared at the Clue Crew.

"First of all," Kitty said, "those cans you dropped are not spray paint."

"What are they?" Bess wanted to know.

Kitty was about to reply when Mr. Stanley cried, "Take it outside, girls! It's a circus in here!"

"Let's go," George said. "But not without these."

George scooped up the cans. Nancy still held Kitty's backpack as the six girls made their way out of the theater. Still sitting outside was the ticket man. He was busy reading a newspaper, not knowing what was happening inside.

Lifting one can, George read the label. "It says 'Color Spray . . . Chalk,'" she said.

"Chalk?" Nancy repeated.

"Yellow, purple, and pink," George added.

"So that's what you used to paint the dogs?" Nancy asked the Kitty Klub. "Spray-chalk in a can?"

"No way!" Kitty insisted. "We didn't even know Helga and Horatio were painted."

"Then what were you doing behind the mansion," Nancy asked, "with cans of colored spray-chalk?"

"We did something sneaky," Ally admitted, "but not what you think."

"What did you do?" Bess asked.

The Kitty Klub looked at one another and giggled.

"Go behind Mayor Strong's mansion," Kitty told the Clue Crew, "and see for yourself."

"Hey, girls," the ticket man called. "You're missing the cat circus!"

Ally smiled at her friends. "He's right. The cats are probably finished with their tuna break. Let's go back in."

"Not without my backpack," Kitty said,

holding out her hand. "And our spray-chalk, please."

George frowned as she stuffed the cans back in the backpack. Nancy handed it to Kitty and said, "Thanks."

The Clue Crew watched the Kitty Klub file back into the theater.

"Maybe we should go back inside too," Nancy said, "To get Chip's pupcakes and help clean up the tuna."

"My mom has plenty more pupcakes," George promised. "And I'll bet the cats are doing a great job cleaning up the tuna."

"Okay," Nancy said as they walked away from the theater. "But I wonder if the Kitty Klub told us the truth about the spray-chalk. What if they really did use it to color the dogs?"

"They only had three cans," George pointed out. "There were more colors on the dogs."

"But Ally said they did something sneaky," Bess said. "What do you think it was?"

"Let's do what Kitty told us to do," Nancy

said. "Let's go back to the mayor's mansion and see for ourselves."

Nancy, Bess, and George all had the same rules. They could walk anywhere up to five blocks as long as they were together. Since the Clue Crew was always together anyway, it was no problem!

This time the girls took a different route to the mayor's mansion. They walked up a sidewalk that led past the back lawn. There they found exactly what they were looking for. . . .

"Whoa!" George exclaimed.

Sprayed across the sidewalk with bright-colored chalk were the words "Cats Rule! Dogs Drool!," "Kitty Power!," and "Meow-Meow, not Bow-Wow!"

"Purple, pink, and yellow," Nancy pointed out. "The same colors that were in the cans."

"So this is the sneaky thing the Kitty Klub did," Bess said. "They sprayed the sidewalk—not the dogs."

"There's nothing wrong with sidewalk chalk,"

George said with a shrug. "But who knew it came in a can?"

Nancy pulled out her clue book and crossed the Kitty Klub off of their suspect list. "That leaves us with the glam squad from Va-Va-Groom," she said.

"Should we go to Va-Va-Groom next?" Bess asked.

"You guys can, but I'm going home," George said. "After a dog wedding and a cat circus, I need an electronic game break."

"I have to go home too," Nancy said with a smile. "It's the second Saturday in the month, so that means pizza night!"

"Cool!" George said. "What do you like on your pizza?"

"Pepperoni, extra cheese," Nancy said with a smile at Bess. "Anything but tuna!"

"You wouldn't believe what Helga and Horatio looked like at their wedding today," Nancy said as she picked up a gooey, cheesy pizza slice. "Like rainbow snow cones!"

Nancy, her dad, and Hannah Gruen sat in their favorite booth at their favorite pizza place eating a pie with three toppings—pepperoni, mushrooms, and extra cheese.

"I heard what happened to those poor dogs," Hannah said. "Who would have done such a thing?"

Hannah was the Drews' housekeeper, but much more like a mother to Nancy. She made sure Nancy ate a good breakfast, did her homework after school, and tucked a napkin in her shirt when she ate cheesy pizza slices!

"The glam squad from Va-Va-Groom was mad that Mrs. Ainsworth used a fancier groomer," Nancy said. "So we're pretty sure they did it."

"They sound like good suspects, Nancy," Mr. Drew admitted. "But you know what I always say."

Mr. Drew was a lawyer but liked to help Nancy with her cases. "Before you accuse anyone of something," he said, "you need solid proof."

"And you need a napkin, Daddy," Nancy said, and giggled as she pointed to a blotch of tomato sauce on her father's shirt. "I'll get some napkins!"

Nancy headed to the counter with the napkins, straws, and jars of spices. On her way she noticed kids sitting at different tables wearing tie-dyed T-shirts.

Maybe tie-dye is a thing this spring, Nancy thought, *or maybe I'm just noticing it because of Helga and Horatio.*

Nancy forgot about the shirts as she approached the counter. Standing there with their backs toward her was a couple dressed in familiar smocks. Right away Nancy knew who they were. . . .

"Kelly and Kevin!" Nancy whispered to herself.

The glam squad sprinkled oregano and garlic on their slices as they spoke to each other. Nancy inched closer to hear. What she got was an earful:

"Mission accomplished, Kelly," Kevin said. "That idea of yours was brilliant!"

"Mrs. Ainsworth is going to wish she hired us to groom Helga and Horatio," Kelly said happily. "That's for sure!"

Nancy's jaw dropped. Did she just hear what she thought she heard? Before Kelly and Kevin could turn around, she hurried back to her dad and Hannah.

"I got it!" Nancy said excitedly. "I got it! I got it!"

"The napkins?" Mr. Drew asked.

"No, Daddy," Nancy said with a smile. "Proof!"

Chapter

6

HIDE AND REEK

The next morning was Sunday but the Clue Crew was already on the case. Together they headed toward Main Street and the Va-Va-Groom dog salon.

"My dad said it's okay to ask Kelly and Kevin some questions," Nancy told Bess and George. "As long as we ask nicely."

"We're always nice," Bess said, before giving George a sideways glance. "Well . . . two out of three of us are."

"Ha-ha," George said with a smirk. She turned to Nancy and asked, "If we're going to question Kelly and Kevin, why are you bringing Chocolate Chip?"

Nancy smiled as her chocolate Lab puppy tugged at her leash. "So we can get inside, that's why," she answered. "Va-Va-Groom is a dog salon, and Chip is a dog!"

Chip stopped tugging to bark at a butterfly.

"She sure is!" Bess giggled.

As the Clue Crew neared Main Street they discussed their plans.

"We won't just question Kelly and Kevin," Nancy said. "We'll also look for clues."

"What kind of clues?" Bess asked.

"Like fur paint," Nancy replied.

"And if they have lots of different colors," George said with a frown, "we'll know they painted the pooches."

"Like that!" Bess exclaimed. She pointed to a large standard poodle walking out of Va-Va-Groom with her owner. All over her shiny black fur were pink hearts. "Sooooo pretty!"

Nancy, Bess, and George entered the salon. A woman stood behind a glass desk, watering a purple orchid. Also on the desk was a gold-framed sign.

"Uh-oh," George whispered. "The sign says 'By Appointment Only.'"

"How can we look for clues if we can't get inside?" Nancy whispered.

The woman stopped watering to smile at Chip. "That must be our ten thirty chocolate Lab," she said. "Wait there, please."

The Clue Crew watched the woman press a button on the wall. Almost right away a man

stepped out from behind a beaded curtain. He was dressed in the usual Va-Va-Groom smock.

"Hello, I'm Perry," he said, "I'll be your dog's attendant today."

"Actually, we'd like to talk to Kelly and Kevin," Nancy said quickly, "if they're here."

"Kelly is in the middle of a pawdicure and Kevin is applying a furry facial," Perry said. "You can wait with your dog in her special suite until it's time for her treatment."

Nancy, Bess, and George traded looks. Clearly the receptionist and Perry mistook Chip for another dog. But if it meant getting inside the salon to look for clues—

"Thanks, Perry!" Nancy blurted.

Perry held Chip's leash as he led the girls down a hall.

"Just so you know," he told them, "we have a brand-new scent in our aromatherapy room."

"I know what aromatherapy is!" Bess said with a smile. "It's when something smells so good it makes you feel good."

"What does your new smell smell like?" Nancy asked.

"Sweaty socks," Perry replied.

"Sweaty socks?" the girls repeated in unison.

"Dogs love the smell of sweaty socks," Perry said, a bit huffily. "You were expecting roses?"

Farther down the hall were rows of doors, each with a time marked on it. He stopped at the door marked ten thirty and swung it open.

"Wow!" George exclaimed as they stepped inside.

Nancy couldn't believe her eyes as they looked around. Inside the carpeted suite was a flat-screen TV, wicker baskets filled with chew toys, a doggy treadmill, a blue-velvet dog-size sofa, and two crystal dishes—one with water and the other with kibble!

"Get your dog settled and make yourselves comfortable," Perry said, turning on the TV to a cartoon. "I'll be back when the barky bubble bath is ready."

Perry left, shutting the door. Bess plopped

down on the velvet sofa, kicking up her feet.

"What are you doing, Bess?" George asked.

Bess pointed up at the TV. "I want to watch *Danger Dog*!"

"Not now," Nancy said. "We have to look for clues before Perry comes back for Chip. I didn't get permission from Daddy for a doggy make-over."

Chip took Bess's place on the velvet sofa. Nancy gave her puppy a piece of kibble, then left the suite with her friends.

Walking up the hall they saw more doors, but

at the end they saw a sign reading: TREATMENT ROOMS, STAFF AND DOGS ONLY. The arrow on the sign pointed down another hall. Quietly the girls peeked around the corner.

"There's more than treatment rooms down that hall, you guys," Bess whispered excitedly. "I spy with my little eye shelves filled with beauty supplies!"

"For dogs, I'm sure," George said. "Maybe that's where they keep the fur paint!"

As George moved down the hall Nancy said, "Wait! The sign says 'Staff Only.' And dogs."

"Then—woof!" George said, before sprinting down the hall. Nancy and Bess rushed after George to the beauty shelves. On them were all kinds of canine beauty products, like glittery paw-nail polish, doggy dazzler stick-on jewels— even hair and tail extensions in hot colors!

"Look!" Bess said, picking up a jar. "Pulverized kibble scrub!"

"Whatever happened to good old belly rubs?" George asked. "This place is weird."

The girls examined every product on the reachable shelves. There were doggy shampoos, even bow-wow body splashes, but no fur paint.

"Maybe the paint is on the top shelf," Nancy said. She pulled over a nearby step-ladder and climbed to the top. Seeing a plastic basket filled with jars she cheered, "Yes!"

"Yes what, Nancy?" Bess asked.

"The jars say 'Colorific Canine'!" Nancy said, carefully carrying the basket down the steps. "Fur paint in all different colors."

Bess looked inside the basket and said, "The colors on the dogs were baby blue, hot pink, red violet, and yellow ochre."

"So?" George asked.

"So these colors are periwinkle blue, bubble-gum pink, blue violet, and lemon yellow!" Bess pointed out.

"How do you know, Bess?" Nancy asked.

"Seriously," Bess said, twirling to show off her colorful spring outfit. "Does anyone know color better than me?"

Nancy smiled until she heard voices. Glancing down the hall she saw Kevin and Kelly. The couple stood facing each other, deep in conversation.

When George saw them too she hissed, "Put the cans back on the shelf, Nancy. Kevin and Kelly can't see us snooping around with them."

Nancy looked at the shelves. The only empty spot was on the top shelf where the fur paint basket was.

"There's no time to climb the ladder," Nancy whispered. "We have to hide!"

"Where?" Bess whispered back.

Kelly and Kevin were still talking when Nancy pointed to the closest door. It was marked SNIFF AND SNORE. "In there," she told them. "Quick!"

Still holding the basket of fur paint Nancy opened the door. She, Bess, and George rushed in, letting the door slam shut behind them.

The room was dark but light enough for the girls to see what was inside. There were dogs lazing on cots and wearing crisp white robes. Most snored loudly while others wiggled their legs as if running in a dream.

"I know those are dogs," George said, sniffing the air. "But what's that funky smell?"

Nancy gulped hard. She didn't have to take a whiff to know that the room was filled with a thick, stinky mist. Crazy stinky!

Bess clapped her hand over her mouth to keep from gagging. Her voice sounded muffled as she said, "I think I know where we are. It's the Aromatherapy Room!"

"And the aroma is . . . sweaty socks!" Nancy cried.

Chapter

GLAM OR SCAM?

"Eww, gross!" Bess cried. "It smells like George's room after a soccer game!"

"I thought it smelled familiar!" George said.

One by one the dogs began waking up. Jumping off their cots, they surrounded Nancy, Bess, and George, wagging their tails and nuzzling the basket.

"I like dogs," Nancy said, "but I don't like sweaty socks. I'm out of here!"

"Me too!" Bess cried.

Nancy told the dogs to stay while Bess pushed the door open. Spilling out of the room, the Clue Crew slammed right into Kevin and Kelly. The basket in Nancy's hand pressed into Kevin's stomach, making him grunt, "Oof!"

Kelly shut the door to keep the dogs from running out. "What were you girls doing in our Sniff and Snore room?" she demanded. "It's for dogs only!"

"I can see why," Bess said with a frown. "Or should I say *smell*?"

"And what are you doing with our Colorific Canine?" Kevin asked, pointing in the basket. "Were you going to paint the sleeping dogs?"

"No way!" Nancy said. She looked at Bess and George, who both nodded their heads. They had wanted to question the glam squad. Maybe now was the right time to do it.

Nancy handed the basket to Kelly as she explained. "The doggy wedding at the mayor's mansion was called off yesterday."

"Because the bride and groom went from

snowy white," George added, "to rainbow bright."

"They weren't even unicorns!" Bess declared.

Kelly nodded and said, "We heard what happened to the dogs. And we feel terrible for them."

"Do you?" Nancy asked. "When Mrs. Ainsworth wouldn't let you groom Helga and Horatio, you both seemed pretty mad."

"You were supposed to groom Huey," Bess said, "but he still looked ewie!"

"So you think we painted Helga and Horatio?" Kevin asked. "With our Colorific Canine?"

"We think dogs look great with colorful fur," Kelly admitted, "but we never apply it without the owner's okay."

"When Huey refused to be groomed we had an idea," Kevin explained. "Since the dog wedding was to bring attention to Waggamuffins, we decided to do just that."

"Do what?" George asked.

"Groom a shelter dog free of charge!" Kevin declared. "We were at Waggamuffins during the time of Helga and Horatio's wedding."

Kevin pulled a mini tablet from his smock pocket. After a few swipes he handed it to Nancy. All three girls looked at a photo of Kevin and Kelly next to a beautifully groomed dog.

"Is that the Waggamuffins dog?" George asked.

Kevin nodded proudly. "Meet Squiggles!" he said. "Kelly and I gave him the full Va-Va-Groom treatment."

"He went from scruffy," Kelly said, "to fluffy!" The couple exchanged excited looks.

"*Scruffy to Fluffy!*" Kevin declared. "That's what we can name our TV makeover show."

"When we finally have one," Kelly added.

While the couple discussed their TV plans, George zoomed out to enlarge the photo.

"Look!" George said, pointing to the picture. "There's a clock on the wall right behind Squiggles, Kelly, and Kevin. The time was one o'clock."

"With the full treatment," Nancy said. "Kevin and Kelly would have been working on Squiggles at the time of the crime."

"The date was yesterday, too," George said, pointing out the photo's time stamp. "Now we know Kelly and Kevin are clean."

"So is Squiggles!" Bess giggled. "Thanks to his very own glam squad!"

Nancy was about to hand the tablet back to Kevin when a voice called, "Yoo-hoo! Girls!"

The Clue Crew turned to see Perry standing at the end of the hall.

"Yes?" Nancy called back.

"Your dog, Sylvia, has just been taken for her beauty treatment," Perry said with a smile.

"Sylvia?" Nancy asked. "My dog's name is Chip. Chocolate Chip."

"Oh my," Kelly said, turning to Perry. "Sylvia's owner canceled her ten thirty appointment this morning. We were so busy, we forgot to tell you."

"Sorry, Perry," Kevin added.

Nancy felt her heart pound. What were they doing to Chip? Stencils? Hair extensions? Glitter paw-nail polish?

"Where's my dog?" Nancy demanded. "Please!"

"Room number seventeen," Perry said with a frown, pointing down the hall.

Nancy, Bess, and George read the numbers on each door as they raced down the hall. Room number 17 had a glass window next to the door.

"Omigosh!" Nancy gasped as they peeked through.

Inside the room was Chip soaking in a frothy bubble bath while getting her back scrubbed.

"How am I going to pay for this?" Nancy groaned.

"We have money left over from the cat circus," Bess said.

"And you got a coupon for this place," George said. "Remember?"

"I remember," Nancy sighed.

After an hour, Chip's beauty treatments were done. As Nancy walked her pampered pup out of Va-Va-Groom she said, "A bath never hurt any dog. But paw polish? How will I explain that to my dad?"

"You won't have to," George said. "How can anyone miss all that gold glitter?"

"Totally glam!" Bess said with a smile. "I love it!"

Nancy spotted two girls from school, Kendra Jackson and Andrea Wu, walking toward them wearing colorful tie-dyed shirts. Just like the ones Nancy had seen the night before.

"Cool shirts," Nancy told them. "What store are they from?"

"We didn't buy them at a store," Kendra replied.

"They're from Bradley Bishop's latest invention," Andrea said.

Bradley Bishop's invention?

Nancy was about to ask Kendra and Andrea about it when a car horn honked.

"That's my mom," Andrea said as the two friends headed toward a parked car. "See you in school tomorrow."

Andrea and Kendra filed into the car. As it drove away George asked, "Wasn't Bradley's latest invention some kind of booth?"

"That's what he said yesterday," Bess said.

Booth? Nancy scrunched her brow thoughtfully. Booth . . . tie-dye . . . Tie-dye booth? That's it!

"Bess, George!" Nancy blurted. "I think I know what happened to Helga and Horatio!"

Chapter

BOOTH OR DARE

The Clue Crew rushed to George's house, hoping to find information on Bradley's booth. Was it a tie-dye booth like Nancy imagined?

"Look up 'Bradley's Brainstorms,'" Nancy told George. "That's the name of his YouView show."

Nancy and Bess peered over George's shoulder as she typed on her computer. Pressing Enter, "Bradley's Brainstorms" appeared on the screen.

"Boom!" George declared. "Now what?"

"Let's watch Bradley's video," Bess said.

"Maybe he's talking about his new invention."

George clicked the arrow and the video played. Bradley was smiling as he walked through what looked like his backyard. He stopped next to a silver pod standing on the grass. The pod was as tall as an adult and had a curtain across the front.

"My latest brainstorm will color your world!" Bradley declared as a smaller boy walked over to the pod. "And here's my brother, Felix, to show you how it works. Step inside the booth, Felix."

"Aww, okay," Felix sighed as he pulled on a pair of goggles. He was wearing a clean white T-shirt and khaki pants.

Felix pulled the curtain aside and stepped through the opening. Bradley pulled the curtain back in place, covering the door and Felix.

"Okay! Let's get this party started!" Bradley said.

The girls watched as Bradley flipped a few switches on the side of the booth. A loud whirring noise rose from the booth—and the sound of Felix shouting, "Whoaaaa!"

"What's going on in there?" George asked.

The noise stopped and Bradley pulled the curtain open. Felix stepped out of the booth. His white T-shirt was splashed with several colors!

"Looking good, Felix!" Bradley said before pointing his finger at the camera. "And so will you, after you rock the Bradley Bishop Tie-Dye Booth!"

Bradley winked at the camera and added, "Available to rent for your next birthday party, school Field Day, or family reunion picnic!"

Excitedly, Nancy turned to Bess and George. "Bradley's latest invention is a tie-dye booth!"

"Yes, but why would Bradley want to tie-dye Helga and Horatio?" Bess asked as Nancy added Bradley to the suspect list.

"Bradley wanted to show off his inventions at the dog wedding," Nancy reminded them. "Maybe tie-dying Helga and Horatio was his way of doing it."

"If Bradley was so proud of his tie-dye booth," George asked, "why wouldn't he stay at the wedding to say he used it on Helga and Horatio?"

"Or film Helga and Horatio for his YouView channel," Bess added.

"Maybe Bradley heard how mad Mrs. Ainsworth was," Nancy said, "and didn't want anyone to know he caused the trouble."

George pointed to the booth on the paused video. "Also, how could Bradley get both dogs inside the booth and return them in enough time for the wedding?"

"Bradley told us he lives around the corner from the mansion," Nancy said. "The dogs had a private door to their room, so he could have snuck in."

"How could Bradley do all that in an hour?" George asked.

"I don't know," Nancy said, "but I do know we need some answers from Bradley."

"Okay," Bess sighed. "But I hope he invented a sandwich-making booth too. It's way past lunch-time and the cats ate all the tuna yesterday!"

The girls went downstairs to the Faynes'

kitchen. There Mrs. Fayne happily fed Nancy, Bess, and George turkey sandwiches and salad.

After a good lunch the girls searched for Bradley's house. When they saw Felix on the porch, they knew they had come to the right place.

"Hi, Felix," Nancy said as they walked up to the porch. "Is Bradley home?"

Felix looked bored as he swung back and forth on a porch swing. "Nah," he replied. "Bradley is at his Junior Inventors' Club."

"Then can we see his tie-dye booth?" Nancy asked.

"Nope," Felix said, while still swinging. "Not unless Bradley is here. And he'd better be home soon because he said he'd play with me."

"We'll play!" George blurted. "Hide-and-seek!"

Nancy turned to look at George. Her brown eyes gleamed—the way they always did when she had an idea.

"You will? Neat!" Felix said, jumping off the swing.

"Cover your eyes and count to one hundred," George said. "Then try to find us."

"A hundred?" Felix cried. "That's a lot of numbers!"

"Unless . . . you don't know how," George said.

Felix's mouth became a grim line. "Sure, I know how. Watch!" he said. Covering both eyes, he began to count, "One . . . two . . . three . . ."

"Let's go," George hissed.

Nancy, Bess, and George raced down the porch steps and around the house to the backyard. Standing in the middle of the yard, just like in the video, was the Bradley Bishop Tie-Dye Booth!

"Look for clues," Nancy told her friends. "Any clues you can find."

The girls circled the booth. Nancy pulled the curtain open a bit to look inside.

"How would Bradley get two dogs to stand still in there," Nancy asked, "while being sprayed with paint, too?"

George slipped past the curtain into the booth. "Maybe Helga and Horatio left some clues. Like painty paw prints on the floor or something."

While George investigated the inside, Bess investigated the outside.

"Look at all these switches on the side," Bess said, pointing to a control panel. "I wonder if one of them opens and shuts the curtain. . . . Maybe this one."

Bess flipped a switch and—*WHIRRRRRRR!*

"Ahhh!" George screamed above the whirring noise.

Nancy gasped when she realized what had just happened. "Bess, you turned on the tie-dye machine!" she said. "George—get out of there!"

"I can't!" George shouted from inside. "The curtain won't open!"

Bess stared at the controls. "And I can't turn it off. I forgot which switch I flipped!"

A hand reached out to flip a switch. It stopped the whirring noise at once. Spinning around, the girls saw Bradley—and this time he looked mad!

Chapter

9

HAPPY BIRTHDAY TO CLUE

"What are you guys doing with my tie-dye booth?" Bradley asked.

"Getting tie-dyed," George grumbled as she opened the curtain with ease and stepped out. "What does it look like?"

George's shirt had been sprayed with vibrant color. So had the back of her neck and hair!

"It was an accident, Bradley," Bess admitted. "We're trying to find out who painted Helga and Horatio before their wedding."

"You wanted to let everyone know about your tie-dye booth," Nancy added, "Since you live right around the corner from the mayor's mansion—"

"You thought I put the dogs in my booth?" Bradley cut in.

"Maybe," Nancy said.

"Maybe not, Nancy," Bess said.

"What do you mean, Bess?" Nancy asked.

"The colors on George don't match the colors on the dogs," Bess explained. "The green on her neck is chartreuse and the pink on her shirt is—"

"Ugly," George interrupted. "You know I don't wear pink."

Bradley sighed as he shook his head. "It's in your hair because you moved the nozzle," he said. "And I did not take those dogs and tie-dye them. Period!"

"How do we know?" Nancy asked.

Bradley pulled a phone out of his pocket. "After I showed you my inventions yesterday I went straight home," he said, "and found this."

The girls watched as Bradley ran the video. It

showed about a dozen kids lined up at his tie-dye booth!

"All these kids heard about my new invention and wanted to try it," Bradley said. "So why would I need to spray two poodles?"

"Bichon frises," Bess corrected.

As Nancy watched the video she noticed something else. Along with the video was the date and time—Saturday, eleven forty-five. It also showed how long Bradley's video ran.

"This video runs for over half an hour!" Nancy whispered to Bess and George. "Bradley couldn't have been recording here and been at the mansion at the same time."

"What are you whispering about?" Bradley asked.

"Your video," George replied. "How come you didn't put this on your YouView channel?"

"I was too busy," Bradley admitted. "Business is booming, you guys!"

Bradley then pointed to George's multicolored hair. "And don't worry about the paint," he told her. "Regular shampoo should get it all out."

"Shampoo? I just washed my hair six months ago!" George cried. When she saw Bess's horrified face she added, "Kidding!"

Nancy, Bess, and George believed that Bradley was tie-dying kids instead of Helga and Horatio.

"Does this mean you'll be too busy with your booth to invent other things?" Nancy asked Bradley.

Bradley shook his head and said, "I've got to strike while the iron's hot. So check out my latest project!"

Pulling a remote from his other pocket, Bradley pressed a button. A rumbling noise suddenly filled the air. The noise came from a toy-size plane perched on the sill of an open window.

Bradley pressed another button. The girls shrieked as the plane swooped back and forth above them while squirting water!

"Meet the Bradley Bishop Garden Gusher!" Bradley said proudly. "Just in time for spring!"

Bradley was having too much fun to stop his

latest invention. Nancy, Bess, and George raced out from under the gushing plane and around the house. Felix was still on the porch, his hands over his eyes.

". . . seventy-seven," Felix counted, "seventy-eight, seventy-nine . . ."

The girls slowed their pace as they walked away from the Bishops' house.

"Go ahead and cross Bradley's name off the suspect list," Bess said.

"I will," Nancy sighed as she pulled her clue book from a soggy pocket. "If it ever dries!"

Nancy, Bess, and George each took a break to go home and change into dry clothes. They met a little more than an hour later outside the park. The Mr. Drippy ice cream truck, a sure sign of spring, was parked outside the gate.

"I hope Mr. Drippy has mint chocolate chip," George said as the girls joined the line outside the truck. "I'd do a headstand on a pyramid for mint chocolate chip."

"I hope this line moves faster!" Bess said, hopping up and down impatiently. "I want a strawberry cone with coconut sprinkles and I want it now!"

Nancy peered down at her open clue book, still damp from Bradley's garden gusher.

"As for me, I want more suspects," Nancy said. "Now that the Kitty Klub, glam squad, and Bradley are innocent, we have no more."

"The case can't be over yet, Nancy," Bess said. "We have to find the pup-painter so Mrs. Ainsworth will support Waggamuffins!"

Suddenly—*WHOOSH!*

Speeding by on a pink scooter was six-year-old Cassidy Ruben. Following on her own scooter was Marcy, Cassidy's older sister and Nancy's friend from school.

"Cassidy, stop!" Marcy shouted. "I want to say hi to Nancy, Bess, and George!"

Cassidy stopped her scooter to turn around. She wore a polka-dotted helmet and T-shirt reading BIRTHDAY GIRL. Also on the shirt was a big number six.

"It's your birthday today, Cassidy?" Nancy asked.

"It was yesterday," Cassidy said. "I wanted to wear my birthday T-shirt again even though it's covered with paint."

"You're the one who wanted a finger-painting party," Marcy told her sister. She turned to George and said, "Tell your mom thanks for sending cupcakes to Cassidy's party. They were yummy!"

"In the tummy!" Cassidy exclaimed, before scooting off again. Marcy gave a little wave and then scooted off too.

"So Cassidy was the six-year-old with the party in the park," George said.

"I'm glad they liked your mom's cupcakes," Bess said.

But Nancy wasn't thinking about cupcakes as the ice cream line inched closer to the truck. She was thinking about what Marcy had just said. . . .

"So Cassidy had a finger-painting party," Nancy said slowly, "in the park . . . yesterday . . . at the same time as the doggy wedding."

"So?" George asked.

"So," Nancy said with a smile as she pointed to her clue book, "the case of the painted pups may not be over yet!"

Clue Crew—and
YOU!

It's your turn to think like the Clue Crew and solve the mystery of the painted pups. Or go to the next page to find out whodunit.

1. The Clue Crew had ruled out the Kitty Klub, glam squad, and Bradley Bishop. Can you think of others with reasons for painting the pups? Grab a paper and pen to write down one or more suspects.

2. When Nancy hears about Cassidy's finger-painting party, it gives her an idea. How could finger paints result in color-dappled doggies? Write some possible reasons on a sheet of paper.

3. The Clue Crew had decided that Helga and Horatio were painted in their room. Where else could it have happened, and when? Using a pen and paper, write down your thoughts.

Chapter

SAVE THE DATE!

"What would a finger-painting party have to do with Helga and Horatio?" Bess asked.

"Think about it," Nancy said. "What if Ludlow did walk the dogs in the park? And what if Cassidy and her friends petted the dogs with paint-covered hands?"

"They'd get wet paint all over the dogs' fur," George said, her eyes wide. "I guess it could happen."

"How can we find out if it did?" Bess asked.

Nancy stepped out of the ice cream line. "Let's go into the park and look for clues," she said.

"But it's almost our turn," Bess complained. "I want to get my ice cream while it's still cold!"

"And I want to solve this case," Nancy said with a smile, "before it gets cold!"

The Clue Crew hurried into the park, heading straight toward the picnic benches where birthday parties were held.

There was no birthday party that day, which made it easier to look for clues.

"Check out what I found!" George called as she pulled a large sheet of cardboard from a trash can. It was a sign with a red arrow and the words TO CASSIDY'S FINGER-PAINTING PARTY, 11:00.

"Eleven o'clock," Nancy said. "That was the time Helga and Horatio were on their walk."

"You mean their run," Bess joked.

The girls checked out each picnic table. Nancy stopped to point at one.

"Look!" Nancy said, "Colorful fingerprints all over the table!"

"The same colors as the paint on the dogs!" Bess said.

Nancy and Bess traded a high five, but George still wasn't sure. . . .

"When we first met Ludlow, he did everything his grandmother told him to do," George said. "Why would he walk the dogs in the park when she said not to?"

"There's only one person who can answer that question," Nancy said as she added the new clues to her clue book. "Ludlow Ainsworth!"

The Ainsworth house was only four blocks away from the park. The girls couldn't believe how much it looked like an old castle!

"Where's the dragon?" George joked.

"I don't know about a dragon," Nancy said, "but there's Ludlow."

Nancy pointed to a boy running across the bright green lawn, tossing a Frisbee at Helga and Horatio. The dogs' tails wagged as they raced to catch it. Two leashes lay a few feet away on the grass.

"Hi, Ludlow," Nancy called as she and her friends walked over.

Ludlow frowned at the sign in George's hand. "Where did you get that?" he asked.

"In the park where the party was," Nancy replied. "Where you might have been too, yesterday, with Helga and Horatio."

"Me?" Ludlow asked, his voice cracking. "Why do you think I was there?"

"Painty hands equal painty fur," George said. "Just saying."

Ludlow shook his head. "I didn't walk the dogs near that finger-painting party," he insisted. "My grandmother told me not to take them to the park, remember?"

Nancy heard a soft growl. She looked down to see Helga and Horatio playing tug-of-war with one of the leashes. She smiled at the dogs' frolics until she noticed something. . . .

"That leash is streaked with paint," Nancy said.

Bess kneeled down for a closer look. "I see fingerprints, too," she said, "In lots of colors."

"So?" Ludlow demanded.

"So if the dogs were wearing their leashes when they got messy," Nancy explained, "it happened on their walk, not in their room."

The Frisbee dropped from Ludlow's hand with a *clunk*. "What are you?" Ludlow asked the girls. "Some kind of detectives?"

"The best!" Bess said with a grin.

While the dogs chewed on the Frisbee, Ludlow heaved a big sigh. "Okay," he said. "I did take Helga and Horatio to the park, but I had a good reason."

"What was it?" Nancy asked.

"I've never had a dog," Ludlow explained. "I wanted to have fun with Helga and Horatio and I wanted them to have fun in the park just like your dog, Chip."

"Oh!" Nancy said, remembering what she told Ludlow.

"I kept Helga and Horatio on the paths," Ludlow went on. "All they did was sniff at a few flowers . . . until a chipmunk ran by."

Ludlow shrugged and said, "The dogs wanted to chase the chipmunk. They tugged at their leashes so hard I lost my grip."

"Did they catch the chipmunk?" Bess asked.

"I don't think so," Ludlow said. "When I found the dogs they were at that birthday party—getting petted and painted!"

Nancy, Bess, and George traded looks. So that's how Helga and Horatio got color-coated. They were right!

"The birthday girl's mom and dad offered to explain everything to my grandmother," Ludlow said. "But I asked them not to."

"Why?" Nancy asked.

"I didn't want her to find out I walked the dogs in the park," Ludlow sighed.

Nancy could tell that Ludlow felt bad. She felt bad too—for Ludlow.

"What happened to Helga and Horatio was an accident," Nancy told him gently. "I'm sure your grandmother would understand."

"Understand what?" a voice asked.

The kids turned to see Mrs. Ainsworth walking over. On her head was a big floppy sun hat. Swinging from one hand was a basket of gardening tools.

"I was just about to pick some spring flowers," Mrs. Ainsworth said. She raised an eyebrow at Ludlow. "Unless something more important happens to be blooming?"

With an encouraging smile from Nancy, Ludlow told his grandmother everything. When he was done he said, "I wouldn't blame you if you're upset."

"Upset?" Mrs. Ainsworth asked with a surprising smile. "Now I know why Helga and Horatio have been so tail-wagging happy since yesterday!"

Ludlow looked puzzled.

"You didn't notice?" Mrs. Ainsworth asked. She nodded at the dogs jumping up at her basket. "That walk through the park did wonders for my melancholy babies!"

"What about their painted fur?" George questioned.

"That stuff washed out like a charm," Mrs. Ainsworth said. "Although I must admit . . . they did look rather glam!"

Nancy felt good to see everybody smile. Even Helga and Horatio seemed to be grinning through their furry faces. There was one important matter to address. . . .

"What about the wedding, Mrs. Ainsworth?" Nancy asked. "Everyone was disappointed that it was called off yesterday."

Mrs. Ainsworth smiled. "Well, now that I know what happened to Helga and Horatio, we can have their wedding next Saturday!"

"Does that mean you'll support Waggamuffins, too?" Bess asked.

"Not only that," Mrs. Ainsworth said with a gleam in her eye, "the shelter dogs from Waggamuffins will be my special guests!"

"All of them?" Nancy asked.

"Sure!" Mrs. Ainsworth said. "The more the merrier . . . or should I say, terrier?"

Mrs. Ainsworth adjusted her hat and said,

"Now if you'll excuse me . . . I have to pluck some pink peonies for the parlor!"

Tails wagging, Helga and Horatio followed Mrs. Ainsworth to the garden.

"You guys really are good detectives," Ludlow told the girls. "You solved this mystery with flying colors."

"Was that a joke?" George asked.

"I guess," Ludlow said, and chuckled.

Nancy, Bess, and George waved goodbye to Ludlow as they walked away from the Ainsworth house. Not only had they solved another case, they made a new friend. And most of all . . .

"Helga and Horatio's wedding will go on after all," Nancy declared.

"I'll tell my mom to bake more pupcakes," George said.

"I'll have a whole week to find something old, something new," Bess said excitedly, "something borrowed—"

"And," Nancy said, holding up her clue book with a smile, "something CLUE!"

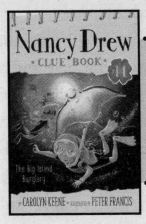

Test your detective skills with even more Clue Book mysteries:

Nancy Drew Clue Book #14
The Big Island Burglary

Nancy Drew and Bess Marvin peered over the side of the boat. The water was so dark, they couldn't see anything below the surface. Bess clutched her life vest and stared at Nancy.

"Do you think there are sharks?" she asked nervously.

"Of course there are sharks. It's Hawaii!" George Fayne called out behind them. She leaned back in her seat and shrugged.

"Stop scaring your cousin," Mr. Fayne said.

"We're all going to be just fine. You think I brought you out here to get eaten?"

Nancy looked off into the distance. Up ahead, a few other boats had anchored in a cove and a bunch of people had jumped into the water. They were all wearing life vests and snorkel masks. As soon as she saw them, Nancy wasn't worried. Some of the kids in the groups looked like they were only six or seven. They were smiling and laughing.

They didn't seem nervous about getting into the ocean at night.

"What do the manta rays look like?" George asked their boat's captain. "Are they gray like sting rays?"

Captain Tane shook his head. "They're black and white. They have spots on their bellies and huge mouths. That's how they eat the plankton."

"What's plankton?" Nancy asked. She'd heard that word before but realized she didn't really know what it meant.

"Plankton is what a lot of the big fish feed on,"

Captain Tane said, scratching his goatee as he steered the boat. He was a round man with thick black hair. "It's lots of tiny sea creatures—eggs and little crustaceans. They're so small, you can't see them."

"Can the manta rays' tails hurt us? Are they sharp?" Bess asked. She was still staring into the water, looking worried.

"Nah. They don't have barbs or stingers. The mantas are gentle creatures," Captain Tane said. "They're called the 'butterflies of the ocean.' I think you're going to love them."

That seemed to make Bess feel better. Ku, the first mate, passed her a pair of flippers, and she sat down on the bench to put them on. Soon their boat was gliding into the cove to join the others.

Nancy had only been snorkeling once before, with her dad. When George's parents invited her on their summer vacation to Hawaii, she knew it would be the first for a lot of things. From the moment they stepped off the plane, it had been nonstop fun. They were staying on the Big Island, which was just like its name—the biggest island in the Hawaiian island chain—and there was so much to do and see. On Sunday, they'd taken surfing lessons. Nancy had even managed to get up on the board and surf a tiny wave all the way to shore. Then Mrs. Fayne took them on a long hike through the jungle. It was so green and beautiful, Nancy felt like she was walking through a movie set. Tomorrow, they were going to a luau, which was a special Hawaiian feast.

That night, Mrs. Fayne and Scotty, George's three-year-old brother, stayed back at the hotel. Scotty was way too young to swim with manta rays, and Mrs. Fayne seemed happy to have an excuse not to go. Nancy wondered if she was as nervous as they were about getting into the water at night.

"What are those for?" Mr. Fayne asked.

As they got closer, they could see that each group had a guide and a surfboard covered in blue lights. The water in the cove was glowing.

"Blue lights attract plankton," Ku said. "The manta rays will swim up for a snack. You just have to hold on to the board. Then you watch and wait."

"Everyone ready?" Captain Tane asked. He parked the boat beside the others.

George was still fiddling with her snorkel, and her dad had to adjust the strap for her. "Ruddy as ull avaa beee," she said through the mask.

Ku climbed down the ladder at the back of the boat and plunged into the water. He was short and muscular, and he was such a good swimmer, he didn't need a life vest. He pulled the surfboard down with him and turned on the blue lights.

"This is going to be great, girls," Mr. Fayne said as he jumped in behind Ku. He grabbed on to the surfboard, which had handles along the sides. They waved for Nancy and her friends to follow.

"Eeeeeeek!" Bess let out a squeal as she jumped in.

Nancy and George climbed down the ladder and swam out to the surfboard. The water wasn't as cold as Nancy thought it would be. All around them, people floated onto their bellies, their masks in the water as they waited for the manta rays.

"Hold on with both hands, just like this," Ku said as he grabbed two handles on the side of the board. He kicked his legs and lay flat.

Nancy and Bess went on one side of the surfboard, and George and her dad went on the other. They stared into the water below. Nancy could hear each of her breaths through the snorkel.

They waited . . . and waited. Nancy started to get a little cold and suddenly wished she'd worn the wet suit Ku had offered her.

All around them, other groups clustered around their surfboards. Just when Nancy was sure nothing was going to happen, she saw something swimming toward them.

"Ahhhhhhhrrrghh!" Bess yelled through her snorkel.

As the creature got closer, Nancy saw its huge, gaping mouth. It was like a giant sting ray. Its mouth was so big, it looked like it could swallow Nancy whole.

Nancy raised her head from the water, suddenly nervous. George and her dad were both still floating on their stomachs and watching the manta. She put her head back down so she wouldn't miss anything.

The creature swam closer and closer, and Nancy's stomach twisted into knots. It was so huge and coming right toward her. When it was a few feet away, it dipped down under them and did a backflip. Its belly was covered with dozens of black spots!

Nancy could see into its gills as it flipped around again and again, taking in huge mouthfuls of plankton. A second manta ray swam up next to it and started doing the same thing. She understood now why people called them "the butterflies of the ocean." They were so graceful. With all their flipping, it seemed like the manta rays were dancing together.

The group kept watching for almost an hour. When the first manta rays swam off, new ones swam over, feeding on the plankton beneath the board. Every minute was better than the last. Ku and Captain Tane had to call Nancy and Bess several times before they picked their masks up out of the water.

"That was incredible!" Bess said.

"Amazing," Nancy agreed.

As they swam back to the boat, Nancy couldn't stop smiling.

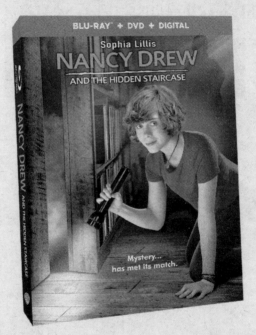
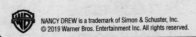

Mermaid Tales

Exciting under-the-sea adventures with
Shelly and her mermaid friends!

Trouble at Trident Academy • Battle of the Best Friends • A Whale of a Tale

Danger in the Deep Blue Sea • The Lost Princess • The Secret Sea Horse • Dream of the Blue Turtle

Trouble at Trident City • A Royal Tea • Tale of Two Sisters • The Polar Bear Express

Wish upon a Starfish • The Crab Ballet • Twist and Shout

MermaidTalesBooks.com

FOLLOW THE TRAIL AND SOLVE MYSTERIES WITH FRANK AND JOE!

HardyBoysSeries.com

Nancy Drew and the Clue Crew®
Test your detective skills with more Clue Crew cases!

Visit NancyDrew.com for the inside scoop!

From Aladdin · KIDS.SimonandSchuster.com